To my mother, Roberta Loomis, and her dreams

C. L.

For Danny, Rama, and little Tomer with love

O. E.

PUFFIN BOOKS
Published by the Penguin Group
Penguin Putnam Books for Young Readers, 345 Hudson Street, New York, New York 10014, U.S.A.
Penguin Books Ltd, 27 Wrights Lane, London W8 5TZ, England
Penguin Books Australia Ltd, Ringwood, Victoria, Australia
Penguin Books Canada Ltd, 10 Alcorn Avenue, Toronto, Ontario, Canada M4V 3B2
Penguin Books (N.Z.) Ltd, 182-190 Wairau Road, Auckland 10, New Zealand

Penguin Books Ltd, Registered Offices: Harmondsworth, Middlesex, England

First published in the United States of America by G. P. Putnam's Sons, a division of The Putnam & Grosset Group, 1997
Published by Puffin Books, a member of Penguin Putnam Books for Young Readers, 2000

10 9 8 7 6 5 4 3 2 1

Text copyright © Christine Loomis, 1997
Illustrations copyright © Ora Eitan, 1997
All rights reserved

THE LIBRARY OF CONGRESS HAS CATALOGED THE G. P. PUTNAM'S SONS EDITION AS FOLLOWS:
Loomis, Christine. Cowboy bunnies / by Christine Loomis; illustrated by Ora Eitan.
p. cm. Summary: Little bunnies spend their day pretending to be cowboys: riding their ponies,
mending fences, counting cows, eating cow, and singing cowboy tunes until it is time for bed.
[1. Cowboys—Fiction. 2. Rabbits—Fiction. 3. Play—Fiction. 4. Stories in rhyme.] I. Eitan, Ora, date ill. II. Title.
PZ8.3.L8619Co 1997 [E]—dc20 96-43057 CIP AC ISBN 0-399-22625-7

Puffin Books ISBN 0-698-11831-6

Printed in the United States of America
Set in Friz Quadrata

The art was done in gouache on plywood panels.

COWBOY BUNNIES

Christine Loomis

pictures by Ora Eitan

PUFFIN BOOKS

Cowboy bunnies

Wake up early

Ride their ponies

Hurly burly

Start at sunup
Work all day
Roping cows
Tossing hay

Mending fences
On the ridges
Jumping gullies
Fixing bridges

Bronco busters
In the saddle
Whoop and holler
Count the cattle

Cowboy bunnies
On the ground
Start the campfire
Gather round

Ring the lunch bell
Rub their bellies
Eat up flapjacks
Eggs and jellies

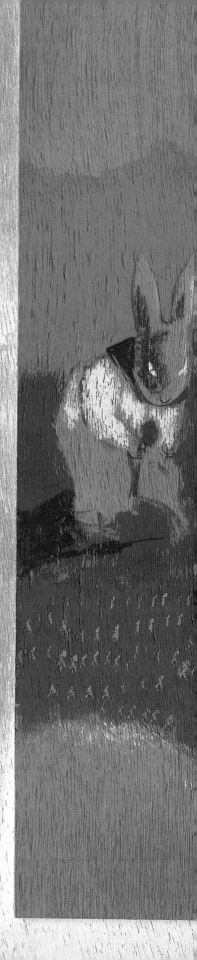

Steak and 'taters   Corn and cake

Bunnies get   A bellyache

Cowboy bunnies
Feeling hot
Find a cool
And shady spot

Chase each other
Sit and doze
Roll their pants up
Dip their toes

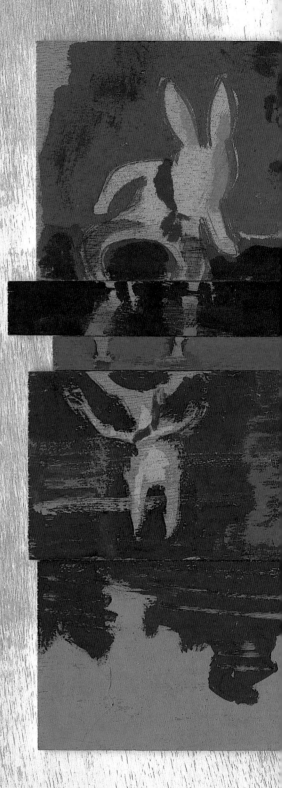

Call their ponies
Hit the trail
Over hill
And over dale

Till their work
Is finally done
Then the bunnies
Have some fun

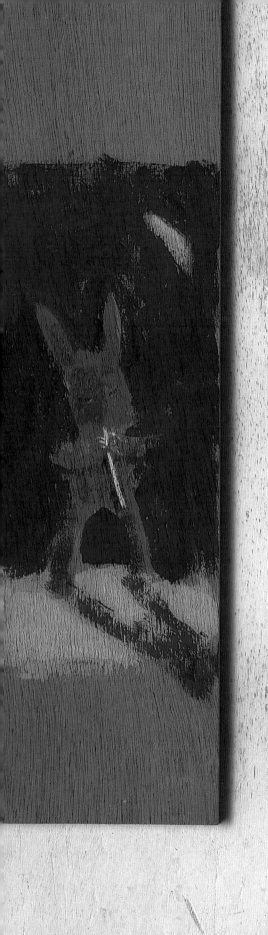

Cowboy bunnies
Big and little
Pick a banjo
Play a fiddle

Grab a partner
Little or big
Dance to the music
Jiggity jig

Sing a lonesome
Cowboy tune
Underneath a
Silver moon

Stay up late   Home they go

Rub their eyes   With sleepy sighs

Cowboy bunnies   In pajamas   Hug and kiss

Their cowboy mamas

Mamas sing
Sweet lullabies
Papas softly
Harmonize

Stars are twinkling
Stars are bright
Cowboy bunnies
Say good night